NINER

AND THE MYSTERY SPACESHIP

Tony Bradman

Illustrated by Martin Chatterton

HAPPY CAT BOOKS

Published by
Happy Cat Books
An imprint of Catnip Publishing Ltd
Islington Business Centre
3-5 Islington High Street
London N1 9LQ

This edition first published 2007
1 3 5 7 9 10 8 6 4 2

Copyright © Tony Bradman, 2007
Illustrations © Martin Chatterton, 2007

A CIP catalogue record for this book is available from the
British Library

ISBN   978-1-905117-42-0

Printed in Poland

www.catnippublishing.co.uk

CONTENTS

Pots of Trouble

As soon as the cabin door slid open, Tommy Niner realized something was badly wrong. He could tell at a glance that Dad's precious Arcturan Stink Blooms weren't feeling too good.

After all, one of Tommy's chores during the past few weeks in space had been to water Commander Niner's rare alien plants every day. So he knew them pretty well.

They usually got excited and waved their purple tendrils around when Tommy came in. But today they drooped, listlessly. The stems were withered, and the petals had gone deathly pale.

1

Tommy tried to remember if he'd done anything that might have harmed the plants. He didn't think so, but he couldn't be sure. Besides, Dad was often grumpy at the end of a long patrol.

They'd been away from base for ages on their current mission, too. But now the Stardust was heading for Galactic Council

HQ. They aimed to arrive just in time
for the annual Space Parade.

Tommy could hardly wait. The whole
fleet would be gathering, so he'd be able
to see most of his friends. And there was
a programme of special events to make
it even more fun.

Although *that* was a major part of
Tommy's problem.

Dad had always wanted to win first
prize at the Flower Show. And as no one

had ever managed to grow Arcturan Stink Blooms on a spaceship, he was very confident.

He won't be for much longer, thought Tommy, pressing the intercom switch. He had contemplated keeping quiet about it, but decided that would only make things worse.

"Tommy calling control deck. Come in, Dad. Over."

"I'm afraid your father isn't here at the moment, Tommy," replied Ada, the Stardust's elderly computer. "Can I help?"

"Not unless you're an expert on sick alien flowers. Dad's stupid old pot plants look as if they've had it." There was a silence.

"Ada, did you hear me?"

"I certainly did," said Ada, nervously. "And I think I'd prefer to be left out of this, Tommy. I'll find Commander Niner and send him to you. Over . . . and *out*."

Typical, thought Tommy. Ada might be old, but she wasn't stupid. She knew Dad was bound to be angry, and she didn't want to get caught in any crossfire.

Tommy sighed, and opened a pack of his favourite chewing-gum. He'd nearly run out, but at least he almost had a complete set of the "Space Villains" cards that came with it.

He was reading the latest one when Dad strode into the cabin and went straight over to the Arcturan Stink Blooms. Commander Niner looked so upset Tommy thought he was going to cry.

"Nothing, Dad, honest. I've been watering them just like you told me to, that's all. They were OK yesterday."

"Well, *something* must have happened," said Dad, crossly. "Healthy plants don't start dying for no reason, do they? And stop chewing that ghastly gum!"

Tommy kept his jaw still, but it was no use. Dad seemed to be winding up

to deliver one of his lectures . . . then
the last crew member turned up, and
Tommy was saved. It was Grandad.

"Hello, you two," he said, happily.
"I suppose this means you've already
discovered the surprise."

"*What* surprise?" said Tommy and
Dad together.

"I injected your plants with a
brilliant new fertilizer I invented this
morning. It *must* be working by now!"

② EMERGENCY STOP

Tommy looked at Dad. Commander Niner's face went very red. His mouth began moving, but no words emerged. Tommy almost expected to see steam hissing out of his ears and nostrils.

They should have known, of course. You could always trust Grandad to make a mess of things with his mad inventions. They tried to keep him under control, but didn't have much success.

"Is there a problem?" he was saying now, innocently.

"Only a small one," said Tommy. "Your fertilizer is killing Dad's plants, and he's not very happy about it."

"Impossible," said Grandad with a

sniff. "My formula is perfect. I'll bet
it's *his* fault. He's never really been any
good at that sort of thing. Why, when
he was your age . . ."

"Hold me back," interrupted Dad,
finding his voice at last. "I think I'm
going to strangle him."

Tommy kept the two adults apart,
but they still argued above his head.
Grandad refused to apologize, which
made Dad even more angry. This could
go on for ever, thought Tommy.

Just at that moment the intercom
bleeped.

"Commander Niner," said Ada,

"Not now, Ada," shouted Dad. He turned back to Grandad. "You've gone too far this time, you old twit . . ."

"But this *is* rather important," said Ada patiently. "I might even go so far as to say it was . . . well, quite urgent."

"I don't care," said Dad. "*You* deal with it, all right? That's what you're there for, isn't it?"

"As you wish, Commander," said Ada, briskly. "Just remember, I did my *best* to warn you."

That sounds ominous, thought Tommy.

Dad and Grandad started arguing again, but suddenly there was a deafening noise. Tommy recognized it instantly. Ada had fired every single retro-rocket at once.

And that meant she was slamming on the brakes!

The three of them flew forward as the Stardust screeched to a halt. Grandad shot out of the cabin door into the gangway, Dad walloped into the wall, and Tommy landed on top of him.

They lay there stunned for a while, listening to crashes and smashes as loose objects continued to fall throughout the ship. Tommy eventually stood up and helped Dad to his feet.

"My poor Stink Blooms!" moaned Commander Niner. A heap of plants, soil and broken pots lay in a corner. "You'd  better have a good explanation for this, Ada. Otherwise I'm going to come up and pull out your plug."

"I did try to warn you," said Ada, snootily. "Next time may I suggest you pay a little more attention when I'm on the point of announcing an emergency stop?"

"But why did you have to do it, Ada?" said Tommy. "Is there something ahead of us?"

"Er . . . yes and no, Tommy," said Ada.

"What *is* she talking about?" said Dad.

"I think she's gone senile," muttered Grandad.

"You'd know all about *that*, wouldn't you?" snapped Ada.

"You're dead right," said Dad. "Do you know, he . . ."

Tommy had finally lost his temper. The others shut up, although Dad glared at him. "Thank you. Now, Ada, would you like to tell us *exactly* what's out there?"

13

"I'm sorry, Tommy," said Ada. "But all I know is what my scanners have picked up. It's big, and it's blocking our way. And there's one other thing."

"Yes, Ada?" said Tommy.

"It's . . . invisible."

Adrift in Space

"Let me get this straight, Ada," said Dad. "You're saying you've detected some sort of object that can't be *seen*?"

"Correct, Commander Niner," said Ada. "That's usually what the word invisible means, isn't it?"

"Have you got any idea what it could be?" asked Dad, ignoring Grandad's sniggers.

"None whatsoever," replied Ada. "Now, I'm rather tired, so if you'll excuse me, I intend to close down and take a nap ..."

"Don't you dare!" shouted Dad. 'I'll be on the control deck in thirty seconds, and I want you wide awake!"

"Really!" said Ada. She sounded very annoyed. "Sometimes I think a computer's work is *never* done."

Tommy followed Dad and Grandad out of the cabin, and soon the three of them were in front of the main viewing screen. It showed nothing but stars and the blackness of space.

"Are you *certain* something's there?" said Dad, peering more closely. "You've made mistakes before."

"You can say that again," mumbled
Grandad. "If I had a Galactic Credit for
every time she's taken us to the wrong
place, I'd be a rich man."

"You'd still be ugly and stupid,
though," snarled Ada.

"Hang on a minute!" said Tommy.
"What's that?"

He had noticed a strange blurring
in the centre of the screen. It spread
slowly, blotting out lots of stars, only

 to disappear,
then return more
strongly.

It kept flickering
on and off like the
picture on a dodgy
TV set, but settled
down at last. The object wasn't invisible
any more. And they couldn't take their
eyes off it.

"Wow!" said Tommy. "I've never seen a spaceship *that* big!"

It was enormous, and what's more, it was bristling with weapons. Tommy tried to count all the laser cannons and missile racks, but he soon gave up.

"Holy solar systems! Action stations!"

"There's no reason to panic, Commander," said Ada. "My scanners aren't picking up any energy surges,

so we're probably not going to be attacked."

"Phew," said Grandad. "That's a relief."

"Is there anyone on board, Ada?" said Tommy.

"It's rather hard to tell," said Ada. "But even if there is, they're not following a definite course. In *my* opinion, that ship is adrift in space."

"Maybe the crew needs rescuing," said Tommy, who was beginning to get excited. "Come on, Dad, let's check it out. You never know, we might end up as heroes!"

"Hah!" snorted Dad. "I doubt that *very* much. And there's an awful lot of clearing up to be done ..."

"*Please*, Dad?" said Tommy, putting on his I'm-Such-a-Well-Behaved-and-Wonderful-Son look.

I promise I'll help later.

"What if it's dangerous?" said Dad.

"You haven't thought about that, have you?"

Grandad said he would go as well to look after him. Tommy reckoned it would be the other way around, but he didn't say anything. Dad seemed to be weakening.

"Oh, all right," Dad said in the end. "Just make sure you're back in time for dinner, and be *careful*. Got it?"

"Yes, Dad," said Tommy, although he didn't really take much notice. He was too busy looking forward to doing something interesting for once.

He couldn't have imagined just *how* interesting it was going to be . . .

4 Deep Freeze

"Ready, Grandad?" said Tommy.

Grandad nodded his spacesuit helmet, and Tommy hit the airlock release. The door slid back, and they both floated out of the Stardust.

They fired their jetpacks and flew towards the other ship, which was soon looming above them. It seemed even bigger now they were close to it.

"I think I can see how to get in," said Tommy.

Grandad followed him along the craft's hull until they arrived at a large hatch. Next to it was a red light which winked on and off. Below that was a handle.

Tommy gripped it and pulled. The

hatch swung slowly
back, and they went
inside. Their path was
blocked by another
door, but that proved
to be just as easy to
open.

"Gosh, it's pitch black in here," said
Grandad.

"We'd better use the torch, then," said
Tommy. "You *did* bring it, didn't you?"

"Of course," said Grandad. "You
know you can rely on me, Tommy. I'd,
er . . . just forgotten, that's all."

Grandad fumbled for a few seconds,
and then there was a click. The torch
beam revealed that they were standing
in a wide gangway. Tommy thought it
was very strange.

Every surface was white and
glittering, and things that resembled

huge, twinkling daggers hung from the
ceiling. Tommy suddenly realized they
were icicles.

He unhooked a testing unit from the
tool kit on his belt
and checked the
temperature. It was
100 degrees below
zero.

"Good job our
spacesuits are

sensor

readout

-100

heated," he said. "Otherwise
we'd be blocks of ice by now."

"It's like a deep freeze," said Grandad.
"I wonder if the whole ship is the
same?"

"Well, we won't find out standing
here," said Tommy. "Come on, Grandad.
This way."

For the next hour they explored the
mystery spaceship's empty, icy cabins.
Finally they reached the control deck,

which at first seemed
as dark and frozen as
everywhere else.

Then Tommy heard
something buzzing,
and glimpsed a small
flash of light. A couple
of wires were hanging loose, and one
was sparking against
the other.

"What is it,
Tommy?" asked
Grandad.

"A fault," said
Tommy, tracing the wires
back. "This one leads to the automatic
pilot, which must have failed . . . and this
one to a switch here. That explains it."

"Explains what?" said Grandad,
looking confused.

"Why the ship is adrift in space,

Grandad," said Tommy. "And I'll bet the switch turns on some sort of invisibility device. That's obviously broken down too."

"Good thinking, Tommy," said Grandad. "I'm sure you're right. I would have worked it out for myself given more time ..."

Tommy cast his eyes round the control deck. They came to rest on a door he hadn't noticed before.

He took the torch from Grandad and went across to it.

"... And of course, that still leaves us without the answer to the most important question," Grandad was saying. "Where's the crew? Can you tell me that?"

Tommy pressed a button and the door opened with a grinding, clanking noise. He shone the torch into the darkness beyond. What he saw made him shiver, even inside his warm spacesuit.

"Actually, Grandad, I can," he said. "They're in here . . ."

A Familiar Face

Tommy and Grandad were walking through a vast storage hold filled with row after row of large glass cases. Each contained a deep-frozen alien. The eerie silence made Tommy feel uneasy.

"Do you think they're alive, Tommy?" said Grandad.

"They might be, I suppose," said Tommy.

"I wouldn't want to get into an argument with one, anyway," said Grandad. "Just look at the size of them! They'd make minced space food of you."

Tommy agreed. Even though they were lying there peacefully, their rough skins sparkling with frost, they still

looked amazingly fierce. They were big, muscular, and armed to the teeth.

"Let's carry on, Grandad," said Tommy. He glanced at his watch. "We'll have to go back soon, and I'd like to find out as much as possible before we report to Dad."

"That's fine by me," said Grandad as they moved off. They didn't talk for a while, then Grandad grabbed Tommy's arm. "What's that over there?" he said.

Tommy shone the torch in the direction Grandad was pointing. It was another glass case, bigger than the rest, and standing on a raised platform.

They climbed up and stared at the alien inside. She was at least half a metre taller than the others, and wore a golden spacesuit with a "Z" on the chest.

There was something very familiar about her, thought Tommy . . . Then

he felt as if a comet had just zoomed through his brain, and he remembered.

"Here, hold this," he said, handing Grandad the torch. He pulled the set of "Space Villains" cards from his pocket and started flipping through them.

"Good heavens, Tommy," said Grandad, "I always enjoy playing with you, but this really isn't the time or the place . . ."

"I'm not playing, Grandad," said Tommy. "I'm searching for a vital piece of information – and here it is! I *knew* I'd seen her face before."

"Well, don't keep me in suspense," said Grandad.

"This is the Evil Zarella," said Tommy, reading the card. "She was a notorious space pirate. Her ship was called the Cosmic Vulture, and she disappeared fifty years ago."

"Are you sure it's her?" said Grandad.

"Positive," said Tommy, showing him the picture. "But why is she frozen like this?"

"It beats me, Tommy," said Grandad.

Tommy read a little more, and discovered that Galactic Council forces had been closing in on Zarella just before she'd vanished. Suddenly he realized what she'd done.

"Now I understand, Grandad!" he said. "Things were getting too hot, so she decided they needed to lie low. And what better way to do it than by using an invisibility device?"

Tommy thought they'd gone into deep freeze so they wouldn't be bored while they waited. And that meant there must be a mechanism somewhere to wake them up . . .

"Could this be it?" said Grandad.

SPACE VILLAINS FACT SHEET

Name: The Evil Zarella

Age: 83

Weight: 150 kilos

Home Planet: Zoldar

Spaceship: The Cosmic Vulture

Favourite Weapon: Neutron Megablaster

Hobbies: Torturing small harmless aliens

Last Seen: Escaping from Galactic Council forces fifty years ago

While Tommy
had been talking,
Grandad had
opened a small
panel under
Zarella's glass case.
Inside was a black
button. Grandad reached for it, his eyes
gleaming.

"Grandad, don't!" shouted Tommy.
But it was too late.

 Grandad jabbed
the button. Instantly,
powerful lights came
on above them, and
a loud whirring noise
filled the hold.

Then a line
appeared on top of the glass case . . .

6 Close Escape.

Tommy watched wide-eyed as the
case lid sprang open and white smoke
poured out. Moments later, a tall,
menacing shape rose through the
swirling clouds.

The Evil Zarella got out of the case
and stood stretching, like someone who
had just woken up in the morning.
Huge muscles rippled beneath her
golden spacesuit.

Tommy held his breath . . . then
realized she didn't know they were there.
Luckily she had her back to them.

He mimed "Ssh!" with his finger in

front of his mouth, and jumped softly down from the platform, beckoning Grandad to follow. They started tiptoeing towards the door.

It seemed light-years distant, and they hadn't got very far when Grandad stopped.

"Pssst, Tommy!" he said in a loud whisper. "You'll never guess. I've only gone and left the torch behind!"

"It doesn't matter, Grandad," hissed Tommy.

"Oh, yes it does," whispered Grandad. "That torch belongs to your father, and you know what he's like . . ."

Tommy was going to say they could worry about that later, but the words never left his lips. He and Grandad both jumped as a voice of steel rang through the vast hold.

Tommy turned round, his heart doing somersaults. Zarella was pointing at them. "Well?" she bellowed. "I'm waiting for an answer!"

"I beg your pardon?" said Tommy, trying to stay calm. He looked over his shoulder. "Are you talking to *us*?"

"I'm certainly not talking to myself," said Zarella, indignantly. "How did you get aboard my vessel?"

"Oh, this is *your* spaceship, is it?" said Tommy, smiling. "I'm terribly sorry. Come on, Grandad. I *told* you we were in the wrong place. We'll just be on our way . . ."

"You will not leave until I have interrogated you," said Zarella, opening a second panel beneath her case. She pressed a button, and a siren wailed. "Intruder alert!"

It seemed that every glass case in the hold suddenly sprang open. Tommy looked around desperately as more white smoke poured out – and Zarella's crew came back to life.

"Make for the door, Grandad!" he shouted.

For once Grandad did exactly what Tommy said. The pair of them ran as fast as they could, ducking past Zarella's lumbering warriors. They seemed stiff from their long sleep.

The door to the control deck slid shut behind Tommy and Grandad. A dull clanging began, and Tommy realized that massive fists were pounding on it from the other side.

"What . . . now . . . Tommy?" said
Grandad, who was puffed out.

"I would have thought *that* was
obvious," said Tommy, pulling him
along. "It's time we went home!"

They raced through a ship that was
also waking up. Lights were coming on,
machinery was starting to hum, icicles
were dripping, and there were puddles
in every gangway.

At last they came to the hatch they'd used to get in. Tommy slammed his hand on the switch . . . but nothing happened.

"Oh no!" he said. "They must have got on to the control deck and locked it from there! Stand clear, Grandad."

Tommy whipped out his blaster, aimed at the switch . . . and pressed the trigger. There was a bang, and the hatch flew open. Then they fired their jetpacks and headed for the Stardust.

"That was close," said Grandad.

Tommy didn't say anything. He knew they weren't safe yet . . .

SPACE CHASE

Back on the Stardust, things were very quiet.

"Where's Dad, Ada?" said Tommy. There was no reply. Then he heard her electronic snoring. "Wakey, wakey, Ada, rise and shine! I'm sorry, but you'll have to finish your nap later."

"Fat chance of that," grumbled Ada sleepily. "What's wrong with you, anyway? You sound rather anxious."

"I think I ought to tell Dad first," said Tommy.

"Be like that," said Ada. "See if *I* care."

But she did summon Commander
Niner, who came through the door
wearing his apron. He was also
carrying a bottle of space polish and a
duster, and looked very flustered.

"You couldn't *imagine* how much
havoc one emergency stop can wreak,"
he said. "I've been working since you
left, and I *still* haven't been able to see to
my plants."

"There might be a lot more havoc if

we don't get out of here pretty sharpish, Dad," said Tommy.

"Tommy . . ." said Dad, his eyes narrowing. "What mischief have you been up to now?"

"It wasn't *my* fault, Dad," said Tommy. He quickly explained what had happened on the mystery ship.

". . . And I think we should put plenty of space between us and Zarella."

"I'll be the one who decides what we do, thank you very much," said Dad. "I *am* in charge of the Stardust, after all."

"May I suggest you make your mind up fairly quickly, Commander?" said Ada. "We appear to be under attack."

They looked at the screen. Zarella's spaceship was bearing down on them. It had fired a flight of missiles, and every single gun was swivelling in their direction.

"Perishing planets!" shouted Dad. "Right, Tommy, you take the controls. Grandad and I will try to hold them off with the main lasers. Get us out of here, Ada . . . now!"

"My pleasure, Commander," said Ada, cranking up the engines. "I'd advise you boys to strap yourselves in, though," she added. "This could be a bit of a bumpy ride . . ."

It was, too. Tommy steered while Dad and Grandad shot down the missiles. Explosions rocked the Stardust and white-hot beams from Zarella's cannons zinged past.

"It's no good," said Tommy. "They're gaining on us. Can't we move any faster, Ada?"

"We're going at full speed already, Tommy."

"Got any ideas?" he said, desperately.

"Let me see . . ." murmured Ada. "No, my circuits are a complete blank," she said at last. Tommy didn't say a word. "And I'm afraid we seem to be flying into another little problem."

"Er . . . what sort of problem, Ada?"

"We're heading straight for a gas cloud," Ada said, cheerily. "You know, the kind that's caused by a collision between two asteroids. It's bound to be full of space rocks."

"Oh no, we'll be smashed to pieces in there!" said Tommy. "This calls for a fast change of direction, Ada. You'd better take over the steering."

"I already have," said Ada. "But it's far too late, of course. We'll never get round it now."

"Terrific," said Tommy. "Thanks for letting me know."

"What's going on, Thomas?" shouted

Dad. He'd been too busy zapping Zarella's missiles to listen to Ada.

"Not a lot, Dad," sighed Tommy. "We'll be plunging into a lethal gas cloud any moment, but don't worry about it."

"We'll be *what*?" yelled Dad.

"You'll see," said Tommy.

Solar Pinball

AAaaaaargghhh!!!

They all screamed as the Stardust flew headlong into the gas cloud. Tommy could see nothing in front of them but a silvery mist filled with tumbling dark boulders.

"For heaven's sake, Ada," shouted Dad. "Are you mad? Get the force field up before we hit any of those things. We won't be able to avoid them. There are just too many!"

Tommy realized Dad was right. Up to then they hadn't bothered with their force field for a good reason. It simply wasn't strong enough to stop Zarella's laser beams or missiles.

But with a bit of luck, it might give them enough protection to survive as they ploughed through the space rocks. In any case, Tommy knew it was pretty much their only hope.

"Good thinking, Commander," said Ada. "Let's keep our fingers crossed it's still working. We haven't tried it

out in *ages*, have we? OK, here we go.
Everybody ready? Force field . . . *on*."

"Well?" asked Dad. "What's the
verdict?"

"You can relax," said Ada confidently.
"I'm happy to announce that the force
field is in full operating order. We appear
to be knocking the space rocks for six."

"Thank goodness for that," said
Grandad. "I don't know about you

lot, but somehow I've never fancied ending up splattered all over a lump of splintered asteroid."

"Me neither," said Dad, wiping his forehead. "Anyway, where's Zarella, Ada? Has she followed us in?"

"It's, er . . . difficult to say, Commander," replied Ada. She sounded embarrassed. "I don't *think* she has, but I can't be sure. Something is having a strange effect on my scanners."

"Old age," mumbled Grandad under his breath.

"I heard that," snapped Ada. "And I can only say it's a good one coming from *you*. I know for certain you're ten years older than me, you balding, cross-eyed, toothless . . ."

"Hold on a second," said Tommy, his eye caught by a change on the control panel. "I can't believe how quickly we're losing power. The force field must be using too much!"

"So it is, Tommy," said Ada. "How clever of you to notice. In fact, it's fading very fast. At this rate, there should be some quite nasty impacts . . . at any moment."

There was a sudden juddering  and then another, and another,

"Told you!" said Ada.

With its failing force field, the Stardust had begun bouncing between rocks like the ball on a pin-table the size of a solar system. Tommy held on grimly as they pinged back and forth.

Unfortunately, his stomach couldn't keep up with the rest of him, and soon

he felt very, very
sick. He closed
his eyes and
swallowed, but it
wasn't much help.

"We won't be
able to take . . .
much more of
this . . . punishment," said Commander
Niner through gritted teeth. "Can't
you . . . do anything . . . Ada?"

"Don't be such a party-pooper,"
chortled Ada. "I'm rather enjoying it,
actually. Now I know what you
humans see in roller-
coasters."

Suddenly an alarm
siren blasted out an
ear-splitting
WHOOP-WHOOP-
WHOOP. Tommy

wheeee!

opened his eyes and tried to focus on the control panel. It was covered with flashing warning lights.

"What's . . . happened . . . Ada?" he managed to say.

"Excuse me?" said Ada, distracted. "Oh, nothing much, Tommy. We've sprung a teensy-weensy leak, that's all."

"Quivering quasars!" yelled Dad. "Air pressure . . . dropping!"

"Rather rapidly, Commander," giggled Ada. "I estimate we'll run out of oxygen in precisely one minute and forty-seven seconds . . ."

sticky moments

"Quick ... everyone ... into ... spacesuits!" shouted Dad, as the Stardust continued to bounce through the gas cloud and its boulders.

"Silly me," said Ada. "I should have remembered you lot need air. I must admit I'm glad I'm a computer. By the way, you've only got one minute and twenty-nine seconds left ..."

twenty-eight
twenty-seven
twenty-six...

"No . . . time . . . for spacesuits,"
Tommy said.

He was racking his brains for a
solution, but he couldn't think of a
thing. With a sense of doom, he began
to wonder if this really *was* the end for
the Niners.

"You're right, Tommy," said Ada. "It's
a shame, but you can't win them all.
I'd just like to take the opportunity to
say I've enjoyed working with this crew.
Well, *two* of them, anyway."

"What a . . . cheek!"
said Grandad. "If
I'm going to die .
. . you are too . . .
you useless old
heap of . . . twisted
wires . . . I'll stick
my screwdriver right
up your . . ."

"That's *it*!" said Tommy. One of Grandad's words had given him the answer. It had exploded inside his head like a super-nova. "Where exactly . . . is this leak . . . Ada?"

"By the rear bulkhead, Tommy, about a metre up from the cabin floor. Although I can't see how knowing the leak's *precise* position is going to help. One minute and twelve seconds . . . eleven, ten . . ."

Tommy unstrapped himself and set off for the danger area. But with the ship still crashing crazily between the space rocks, it was almost impossible to stay on his feet.

He lurched from side to side, but for a while he seemed to be making good progress. Then he tripped, fell – and rolled in completely the wrong direction!

"Oh, bad luck, Tommy," said Ada. "It looks like you won't make it now. What were you going to try and do, anyway? I'm intrigued . . . forty-one seconds . . ."

forty
thirty-nine
thirty-eight

Tommy ignored her. He stood up and focused his mind on getting to that leak. Nothing else mattered. He took one

step, two steps, three steps, there was a
CRASH!, the cabin tilted . . .

And he was thrown to exactly the
right place!

It took him several precious seconds
to get himself sorted out, and then
several more to find the leak.
But there it was at last, a
rip in the hull no bigger
than a small keyhole.

Tommy knew he
wouldn't be able to do a proper repair.
For that he would have to weld the
rip shut with a metal
patch. But he did have
something almost as
good. *His space villains'
chewing-gum.*

He tore open his last pack and
popped the gum into his mouth. He
chewed furiously, the seconds ticking

away. Then he finally took it out . . .
and *stuck* it over the hole.

"I'm impressed," said Ada. "I would
never have thought of that. And only
eight seconds to go, too."

"Well done, Tommy!" said Dad,
getting out of his seat to give his son

a hug. Tommy smiled and felt very relieved, not least because for once he hadn't been told off about the gum.

Then he realized the deck was steady beneath his space boots.

"Hey, we've stopped bouncing!" he said. "What's happening out there now, Ada?"

"Don't ask me," she said. "I haven't got a clue."

"As usual," said Grandad.

"Listen, wrinkle-features," snapped Ada, "I don't know what's going on because of this radiation, OK? It's doing terrible things to all my connections."

Suddenly it went very quiet on the control deck.

A Deadly Glow

"I'm terribly sorry, didn't I tell you?"
said Ada. "I've discovered what was
affecting my scanners. This gas cloud
is positively *throbbing* with powerful
radiation."

"What sort of radiation is it?"
asked Dad. Tommy could hear that he
sounded very worried.

"I'm not really sure," replied Ada.
"I've never come across anything like it
before. It's *very* interesting, though," she
whispered, dimming the lights. "Let me
show you."

As the control deck went dark, they
saw that every piece of equipment and
every surface was giving off a faint,
deadly glow. So were Dad, Grandad and
Tommy.

"Hey presto!" said Ada, like a magician performing a trick. "It's rather attractive, isn't it?"

"But will it actually *harm* us?" asked Dad.

"It might . . . and then again, it might not," said Ada. "If you want my advice, you won't hang around to find out. It's already done something peculiar, so it *could* do something else."

"You know, I had a bad feeling about today from the moment I got up," said Grandad. "Maybe I should have stayed in bed."

"I wish you'd stay there all the time," growled Ada. Grandad opened his mouth to argue, but Ada swept on. "Shall I take us out of here then, Commander Niner?" she said.

"Just hold on a minute," said Dad, a strained expression on his face. "I need to think . . . I still don't understand why we've stopped crashing into those space rocks."

"Ah, I've worked that one out as well," said Ada.

"Wonders will never cease," said Grandad.

"Belt up and give her a chance, Grandad, will you?" said Tommy. "This is important."

"Sorry I spoke," sniffed Grandad.

"Thank you, Tommy," said Ada. "In fact, it's all very simple. Gas clouds like this tend to have a clear area in their centre. And that's where we are now."

"I get it," said Tommy. "We're safe here, but if we move away from this spot we'll start hitting boulders again. Right, Ada?"

"I couldn't have put it better myself,"
Ada said. "We should be able to make
it, though. I've managed to recharge the
power cells, which means the force field
is back at full strength."

"Full speed ahead then, Ada,"
said Dad. "The sooner we leave this
radiation behind, the happier I'll be."

"What about Zarella?" said Tommy.

"She can't have followed us in, Thomas," said Dad. "We'd be under attack if she had. No, she's probably looking for a rich planet to raid. It's our duty to warn the Galactic Council!"

Tommy knew Dad was right, although that didn't make the prospect of another trip through the solar pinball any easier. He got strapped in, closed his eyes and took a deep breath.

But this time there were no crashes.

According to Ada, that was because the Stardust had become much heavier, which meant it was much harder to knock off course. She didn't know where the extra weight had come from.

Tommy didn't care. He was just glad he and his stomach could travel together. The glow was fading, too . . . But Tommy's good mood vanished when they finally emerged from the gas cloud.

Waiting for them dead ahead was ...
the Cosmic Vulture!

The radio crackled into life, and a
familiar voice of steel rang through the
control deck.

"Prepare to be boarded!" it roared.

And then the Stardust shook as
something gripped it from the
outside ...

74

CAPTURED!

A long tube had emerged from the Cosmic Vulture and clamped itself to the Stardust. Then a big hole was blown in the wall of the control deck, which became filled with choking smoke.

A squad of warriors poured through, followed by the fierce figure of the Evil Zarella herself. She towered over the coughing Niners, who got out of their seats and raised their hands.

"So, we meet again," said Zarella with an evil smile. Her eyes were on Tommy, but he didn't smile back. "You rushed off so quickly last time we didn't have a chance to talk."

"You'll get nothing from me, Zarella," said Tommy as the smoke cleared. "I know you're evil. I've read all about you."

"It's so nice to be remembered," she said. "Not that I intended to stay frozen this long. It was only supposed to be for a few months, but one of my crew set the timer wrong."

"There's someone like that on the Stardust," said Ada. "He ruins everything he lays his hands on."

"Take that back, you . . ." Grandad started to say. But Zarella pointed her blaster at him, and he shut up.

"Tell me more," said Zarella. Tommy was surprised. She was speaking in a silky-smooth voice. "You seem to have had a lot to put up with. But a ship's computer always does, doesn't it?"

"How true," said Ada, who was practically purring by now.

Tommy had to admit Zarella was pretty good at extracting information. A few minutes of flattering chat with Ada gave the villain everything she wanted to know.

And when she heard about the Space Parade, her eyes lit up.

"The whole fleet will be there, you say?" she murmured. "Perfect. Now my invisibility device has been fixed, I can sneak up on them and destroy all my enemies at one stroke."

"You'll never get away with it," said Tommy.

"Oh no?" said Zarella, the steel creeping back into her voice. "But I *will*. And then the galaxy will be at my mercy!"

"Suffering sun-spots, Ada," muttered Dad. "When are you going to learn to keep that big mouth of yours shut?"

"Charming," squawked Ada. "That's no way to talk to a computer of my age, I must say. Why . . ."

"Be quiet, machine," said Zarella menacingly, waving her blaster at Ada now. "I wish to speak with the handsome one I had not noticed before. Tell me, what is *your* name?"

"Er . . . Commander Niner," said Dad, nervously. Zarella had come over to examine him more closely. "And I must

protest about your unprovoked attack on a Galactic Council ship."

"Umm, yes," Zarella said. "I will allow you to become my fifth husband. Guards, take him to my quarters."

"What?" squeaked Dad, blushing to the roots of his hair. "I'm very honoured, of course, but . . ." Then he paused as something occurred to him. "What happened to the other four?"

"Ah, they suffered . . . *tragic* accidents," said Zarella.

Tommy wondered what Zarella had lined up for Grandad and him. It was bound to be something nasty if her plans for Dad were anything to go by. Tommy just felt glad he wasn't a grown-up.

"Help!" yelped Dad as Zarella's

warriors tried to drag him away. "Do something, Tommy!"

Tommy didn't know what to do. He *had* to save his family and the entire galaxy — but *how*? He looked round desperately . . . and then his eyes fell on the control deck door.

There was a small window, and through it Tommy could see lots of purple things waving at him.

Suddenly he realized what they were, and smiled . . .

Purple Panic

Everyone else was concentrating on Dad's struggle with Zarella's guards. So Tommy wasn't spotted edging towards the door. He pressed the switch, and it slid open.

Beyond it was a mass of twitching vegetation.

Tommy had worked out that the purple things were Dad's plants. They had obviously survived after all, and what's more, the radiation must have had an effect on Grandad's fertilizer.

Judging by the size of the plants that came waddling on to the control deck,

it had become the best fertilizer ever. They were *much* bigger than the Evil Zarella and her warriors.

There were dozens of them as well. Tommy understood now where that extra weight on the Stardust had come from. Dad's Arcturan Stink Blooms had been breeding like mad.

"What trickery is this?" said Zarella, backing away.

"It's no trick, Zarella," said Tommy. "These plants are our secret weapon. You should never have taken on the Niners, you know. We've got . . . flower power!"

Tommy stepped aside as the Stink Blooms advanced. The sight of Dad being held captive

seemed to have made them very angry. They did a lot of rustling, and their tendrils went berserk.

Zarella and her guards started firing their weapons, and soon the control deck was the scene of a mighty battle. The air was filled with crackling laser beams, cries and screams.

Tommy dived for cover, pulling Grandad with him.

"Any sign of Dad, Ada?" shouted Tommy above the din.

"Don't worry, Tommy," said Ada. "I think he's all right."

Tommy took the risk of peeking, and saw an amazing spectacle. One of the plants had picked up the two warriors who had been holding Dad, and was banging them together, very hard.

Dad, meanwhile, was crawling off to hide under a table.

"That's *awesome*," said Tommy. "They're unstoppable."

It seemed Zarella was beginning to agree. There was a distinct look of panic on her face.

"Fall back!" she called out. "Retreat!"

But she and her troops were cornered, and it wasn't long before they were forced to surrender. For the first time in her wicked career, the Evil Zarella had been defeated . . .

. . . By a bunch of pot plants!

Dad still wasn't satisfied, though. After they'd disarmed Zarella and her warriors and locked them up, he stood on the Stardust's battered control deck looking depressed.

"This place is a complete wreck," he moaned. "I'll *never* get it cleared up."

"Cheer up, Dad," said Tommy. "There *is* a bright side to this, you know. We'll be heroes when we hand over Zarella at HQ."

"Good point, Thomas," said Dad, brightening. "I hadn't thought of that."

"But what are you going to do with these plants?" said Grandad, trying to shake off one that was being a little too friendly. "They're everywhere. The ship

is *packed* with them."

"That's no problem either," said
Tommy. "They're bound to win first
prize at the Flower Show, aren't they?"

"Of *course* they are," said Dad, smiling
broadly now. "I'll just go and see if my
best spacesuit needs ironing . . ."

"Tommy," said Ada after Dad had gone, "do you think I ought to tell Commander Niner we've already missed the Flower Show?"

"Ah, I wouldn't if I were you," said Tommy. "Let's keep him happy for a while . . ."